A STORY OF THE FOREST

HANSEL AND GRETEL

A STORY OF THE FOREST

BY WILLIAM & JACOB GRIMM

MUSIC BY ENGELBERT HUMPERDINCK

AND ILLUSTRATIONS BY WARREN CHAPPELL

Published by ALFRED A. KNOPF, New York

The four selections from the score of the opera *HANSEL & GRETEL* by Engelbert Humperdinck, have been especially arranged for easy playing by Miss Elizabeth Quaile, and the autographing done by Maxwell Weaner.

This title was originally catalogued by the Library of Congress as follows:

Grimm, Jakob Ludwig Karl, 1785–1863.
 Hansel and Gretel, a story of the forest, by William & Jacob Grimm; music by Engelbert Humperdinck and illustrations by Warren Chappell. New York, A. A. Knopf, 1944.

 ₍32₎ p. incl. col. front., col. illus. 19½ x 25 cm.

 "First edition."

 I. Grimm, Wilhelm Karl, 1786–1859, joint author. II. Chappell, Warren, 1904–   illus. II. Humperdinck, Engelbert, 1854–1921. Hänsel und Gretel. IV. Title.

PZ8.G882Ha 16   44—9580

Library of Congress   ₍63v¾₎

Trade Ed.: ISBN: 0-394- 81221-2   Lib. Ed.: ISBN: 0-394- 91221-7

HANSEL & GRETEL

ARD BY A GREAT FOREST dwelt a poor wood-cutter with his wife and his two children. The boy was called Hansel, and the girl Gretel. He had little to bite and to sup, and once when great scarcity fell on the land, he could no longer procure daily bread. When he thought this over by night in his bed, tossing about in his anxiety, he groaned and said to his wife, "What is to become of us? How are we to feed our poor children, when we no longer have anything even for ourselves?"

"I'll tell you what, husband," answered the woman, "early tomorrow morning we will take the children out into the forest to where it is the thickest;

there we will light a fire for them, and give each of them one piece of bread more, and then we will go to our work and leave them alone. They will not find the way home again, and we shall be rid of them."

"No, wife," said the man, "I will not do that; how can I bear to leave my children alone in the forest? The wild animals would soon come and tear them to pieces."

"Oh, you fool!" said she, "then we must all four die of hunger; you might as well plane the planks for our coffins," and she gave him no peace until he consented.

"But I feel very sorry for the poor children, all the same," said the man.

The two children had also not been able to sleep for hunger, and had heard what their step-mother had said to their father. Gretel wept bitter tears, and said to Hansel, "Now all is over with us."

"Be quiet, Gretel," said Hansel, "do not distress yourself; I will soon find a way to help us." And when the old folks had fallen asleep, he got up, put on his little coat, opened the door below, and crept outside. The moon shone brightly, and the white pebbles which lay in front of the house glittered like

Brother, Come and Dance

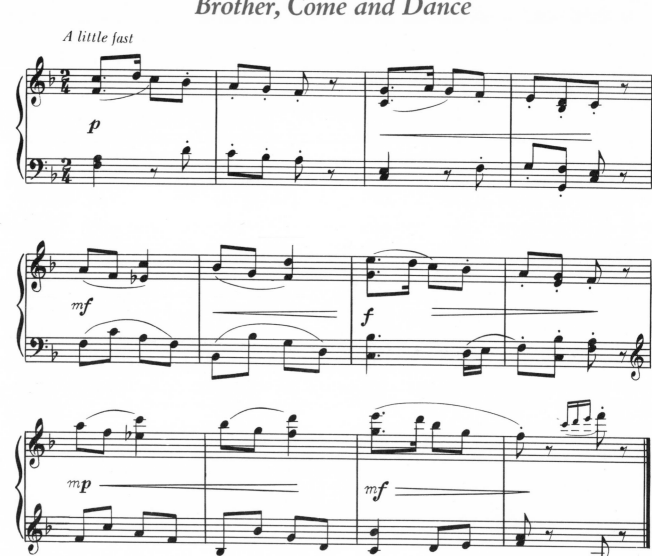

real silver pennies. Hansel stooped and put as many of them in the pocket of his coat as he could possibly get in. Then he went back and said to Gretel, "Be comforted, dear little sister, and sleep in peace, God will not forsake us," and he lay down again in bed.

When day dawned, but before the sun had risen, the woman came and awoke the two children, saying, "Get up, you sluggards! We are going into the forest to fetch wood." She gave each a little piece of bread, and said, "There is something for your dinner, but do not eat it up before then, for you will get nothing else."

Gretel took the bread under her apron, as Hansel had the stones in his pocket. Then they all set out together on the way to the forest.

When they had walked a short time, Hansel stood still and peeped back at the house; he did it again and again.

His father said, "Hansel, what are you looking at there? Mind what you are about, and do not forget how to use your legs."

"Ah, father," said Hansel, "I am looking at my little white cat, which is sitting up on the roof, and wants to say good-bye to me."

HANSEL & GRETEL

The wife said, "Fool, that is not your little cat, that is the morning sun shining on the chimneys." Hansel, however, had not been looking back at the cat, but had been constantly throwing the white pebbles out of his pocket on the road.

When they had reached the middle of the forest, the father said, "Now, children, pile up some wood, and I will light a fire so that you will not be cold." Hansel and Gretel gathered brushwood together, as high as a little hill. The brushwood was lighted, and when the flames were burning very high the woman said, "Now, children, lay yourselves down by the fire and rest; we will go into the forest, and cut some wood. When we have done, we will come back and fetch you away."

Hansel and Gretel sat by the fire. When noon came, each ate a little piece of bread, and as they heard the strokes of the axe they believed that their father was near. It was, however, not the axe, but a branch that he had fastened to a withered tree which the wind was blowing back and forth.

As they had been sitting such a long time, their eyes shut with fatigue, and they fell fast asleep. When at last they awoke, it was already dark night.

HANSEL & GRETEL

Gretel began to cry, and said, "How are we to get out of the forest now?"

But Hansel comforted her, saying, "Just wait until the moon has risen; then we will soon find the way."

And when the full moon had risen, Hansel took his little sister by the hand, and followed the pebbles, which shone like newly-coined silver pieces, and showed them the way.

They walked all night, and by daybreak came once more to their father's house. They knocked at the door, and when the woman opened it and saw that it was Hansel and Gretel, she said, "You naughty children, why have you slept so long in the forest? We thought you were never coming back at all!" The father, however, rejoiced, for it had cut him to the heart to leave them behind alone.

Not long afterward, there was once more great scarcity in all parts, and the children heard their mother saying at night to their father, "Everything is eaten again; we have one half loaf left, and after that there is an end. The children must go, we will take them farther into the wood, so that they will not find their way out again; there is no other means of saving ourselves!"

The Little Man in the Wood

Quietly

HANSEL & GRETEL

The man's heart was heavy, and he thought, "It would be better to share the last mouthful with your children." The woman, however, would listen to nothing, but scolded and reproached him, and as he had yielded the first time, he had to do so now a second time.

The children were, however, still awake, and had heard the conversation. When the old folks were asleep, Hansel again got up, and wanted to go out and pick up pebbles, but the woman had locked the door, and Hansel could not get out. Nevertheless he comforted his little sister, and said, "Do not cry, Gretel, go to sleep quietly, the good God will help us."

Early in the morning the woman came and took the children out of their bed. Their bit of bread was given to them, but it was still smaller than the time before. On the way into the forest Hansel crumbled his in his pocket, and often stood still and threw a morsel on the ground.

"Hansel, why do you stop and look around?" said the father. "Go on."

"I am looking back at my little pigeon, which is sitting on the roof, and wants to say good-bye to me," answered Hansel.

"Simpleton!" said the woman, "that is not your little pigeon, that is the

Children's Prayer

morning sun shining on the chimney." Hansel, however, little by little, threw all the crumbs on the path.

The woman led the children still deeper into the forest, where they had never been before in their lives. Then a great fire was again made, and the mother said, "Just sit there, you children, and when you are tired you may sleep a little; we are going into the forest to cut wood, and in the evening when we are done, we will come and fetch you away."

When it was noon, Gretel shared her piece of bread with Hansel, who had scattered his by the way. Then they fell asleep, and evening came and went, but no one came to the poor children.

They did not awake until it was dark night, and Hansel comforted his little sister, saying, "Just wait, Gretel, until the moon rises, and then we shall see the crumbs of bread which I have strewn about; they will show us our way home again."

When the moon came they set out, but they found no crumbs, for the many thousands of birds which fly about in the woods and fields had picked them all up. Hansel said to Gretel, "We will soon find the way," but they did

HANSEL & GRETEL

not find it. They walked the whole night, and all the next day too from morning till evening, but they did not get out of the forest. They were very hungry, for they had nothing to eat but a few berries, which they found on the ground. And as they were so weary that their legs would carry them no longer, they lay down beneath a tree, and fell asleep.

It was now three mornings since they had left their father's house. They began to walk again, but they got ever deeper into the forest; if help did not come soon, they must die of hunger and weariness.

When it was mid-day, they saw a beautiful snow-white bird sitting on a bough, singing so delightfully that they stood still to listen. And when it had finished its song, it spread its wings and flew away before them, and they followed until they reached a little house, on the roof of which it alighted; and when they came quite up to the little house they saw that it was built of bread and covered with cakes, but that the windows were of clear sugar.

"We will set to work on that," said Hansel, "and have a good meal. I will eat a bit of the roof; you, Gretel, can eat some of the window; that will taste sweet." Hansel reached up above, and broke off a little of the roof to try how

it tasted, and Gretel leant against the window and nibbled at the panes.

Then a soft voice cried from the room,

> *"Nibble, nibble, gnaw,*
> *Who nibbles at my house?"*

The children answered,

> *"The wind, the wind,*
> *The heaven-born wind,"*

and went on eating without disturbing themselves. Hansel, who thought the roof tasted very nice, tore down a great piece of it, and Gretel pushed out the whole of one window-pane, sat down, and enjoyed herself with it.

Suddenly the door opened, and a very, very old woman, who supported herself on crutches, came creeping out. Hansel and Gretel were so frightened that they let fall what they had in their hands.

The old woman, however, nodded her head, and said, "Oh, you dear children, who has brought you here? Do come in, and stay with me. No harm shall befall you." She took them both by the hand, and led them into her little house. She set good food before them, milk and pancakes, with sugar, apples, and nuts. Afterwards two pretty little beds were covered with clean white linen, and Hansel and Gretel, lying in them, thought themselves in heaven.

The old woman had only pretended to be so kind; she was really a wicked witch, who lay in wait for children, and had built the little bread house only in order to entice them there. When a child fell into her power, she killed it, cooked and ate it, and that was a feast day with her.

Witches have red eyes, and cannot see far, but they have a keen scent like the beasts, and are aware when human beings draw near. When Hansel and Gretel came into her neighborhood, she laughed maliciously, and said mockingly, "I have them, they shall not escape me again!"

Early in the morning, before the children were awake, she was already up, and when she saw both of them sleeping and looking so pretty, with their plump red cheeks, she muttered to herself, "That will be a dainty mouthful!" Then she seized Hansel with her shrivelled hand, carried him into a little stable, and shut him in with a grated door. He might scream as he liked; it was no use.

Then she went to Gretel, shook her till she awoke, and cried, "Get up, lazy thing, fetch some water, and cook something good for your brother. He is in the stable outside, and is to be made fat. When he is fat, I will eat him." Gretel began to weep bitterly, but it was all in vain; she was forced to do what the wicked witch ordered her.

And now the best food was cooked for poor Hansel, but Gretel got nothing but crab-shells.

Every morning the woman crept to the little stable, and cried, "Hansel, stretch out your finger; let me feel if you will soon be fat."

Hansel, however, stretched out a little bone to her, and the old woman, who had dim eyes, could not see it, thought it was Hansel's finger, and was astonished that there was no way of fattening him.

When four weeks had gone by, and Hansel still continued thin, she was seized with impatience, and would not wait any longer.

"Hola, Gretel," she cried to the girl, "move along and bring some water. Let Hansel be fat or lean, tomorrow I will cook him."

Ah, how the poor little sister did lament when she had to fetch the water, and how the tears did flow down her cheeks! "Dear God, do help us," she

The Witches' Dance

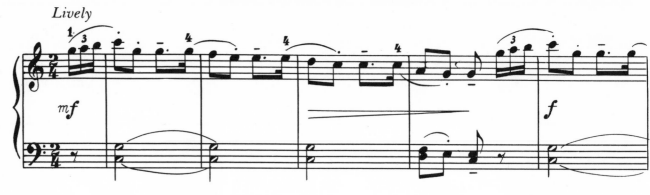

cried. "If the wild beasts in the forest had but devoured us, we should at any rate have died together."

"Just keep your noise to yourself," said the old woman, "all that won't help you a bit."

Early in the morning, Gretel had to go out and hang up the cauldron with the water, and light the fire. "We will bake first," said the old woman. "I have already heated the oven, and kneaded the dough." She pushed poor Gretel out to the oven, from which flames of fire were already darting.

"Creep in," said the witch, "and see if it is properly heated, so that we can shut the bread in." When once Gretel was inside, she intended to shut the oven and let her bake in it, and then she would eat her, too.

But Gretel saw what was in her mind, and said, "I don't know how; how do you get in?"

"Silly goose," said the old woman. "The door is big enough; just look, I can get in myself!" and she crept up and thrust her head into the oven. Then Gretel gave her a push that drove her far into it, shut the iron door, and fastened the bolt.

She howled horribly, but Gretel ran away, and the godless witch was miserably burnt.

Gretel, however, ran as quick as lightning to Hansel, opened his little stable, and cried, "Hansel, we are saved! The old witch is dead!" Hansel sprang out like a bird from its cage. How they did rejoice and embrace, and dance about and kiss each other!

And as they had no longer any need to fear her, they went into the witch's house, and in every corner there stood chests full of pearls and jewels. "These are far better than pebbles!" said Hansel, and thrust into his pockets what-

ever could be got in, and Gretel said, "I, too, will take something home with me," and filled her pinafore full. "Now we will go away," said Hansel, "and get out of the witch's forest."

When they had walked for two hours, they came to a great piece of water.

HANSEL & GRETEL

"We cannot get over," said Hansel, "I see no foot-plank, and no bridge."

"And no boat crosses either," answered Gretel, "but a white duck is swimming there; if I ask her, she will help us over." Then she cried,

"Little duck, little duck, dost thou see,
Hansel and Gretel are waiting for thee?
There's never a plank, or bridge in sight,
Take us across on thy back so white."

The duck came to them, and Hansel seated himself on its back, and told his sister to sit by him.

"No," replied Gretel, "that will be too heavy for the little duck; she shall take us across, one after the other."

The good little duck did so, and when they were once safely across and had walked for a short time, the forest seemed more and more familiar; at length they saw their father's house from afar.

HANSEL & GRETEL

He was coming toward them. Then they began to run, and threw themselves into their father's arms. The man had not known one happy hour since he had left the children in the forest; the woman, however, was dead.

Gretel emptied her pinafore until pearls and precious stones ran about the room, and Hansel threw one handful after another out of his pocket to add to them. Then all anxiety was at an end, and they lived together in perfect happiness.

My tale is done; there runs a mouse; whoever catches it, may make himself a big fur cap out of it.